George M. Baker

My Brother's Keeper

A drama in three acts

George M. Baker

My Brother's Keeper
A drama in three acts

ISBN/EAN: 9783337343842

Printed in Europe, USA, Canada, Australia, Japan

Cover: Foto ©Andreas Hilbeck / pixelio.de

More available books at **www.hansebooks.com**

MY BROTHER'S KEEPER.

A Drama, in Three Acts.

BY THE AUTHOR OF

" Sylvia's Soldier,"
" Once on a Time," " Down by the Sea," " The Last Loaf,"
" Bread on the Waters," " Stand by the Flag," " The Tempter," " A Drop too
Much," " We're all Teetotalers," "A Little more Cider," " Thirty Minutes
for Refreshments," " Wanted, a Male Cook," "A Sea of Troubles,"
" Freedom of the Press," " A Close Shave," " The Great
Elixir," " The Man with the Demijohn," " Humors of
the Strike," " New Brooms sweep Clean," " My
Uncle the Captain," " The Greatest Plague
in Life," " No Cure, no Pay," " The
Grecian Bend," " War of the
Roses," " Lightheart's
Pilgrimage,"
" The
Sculptor's
Triumph," " Too
Late for the Train,"
" Snow-Bound," " The Ped-
dler of Very Nice," " Bonbons,"
" Capuletta," " An Original Idea," " My
Brother's Keeper," " Among the Breakers,"
" The Boston Dip," " The Duchess of Dublin," " A
Tender Attachment," " Gentlemen of the Jury," " A Public
Benefactor," " The Thief of Time," " The Hypochondriac," " The
Runaways," " Coals of Fire," " The Red Chignon," " Using the Weed,"
" A Love of a Bonnet," " A Precious Pickle," " The Revolt
of the Bees," " The Seven Ages,"
&c., &c., &c.

BOSTON:

GEORGE M. BAKER & CO.,

149 WASHINGTON STREET.

MY BROTHER'S KEEPER.

A DRAMA IN THREE ACTS.

CHARACTERS.

ABEL BENTON, Merchant.

MATTHEW ALLEN,
RICHARD CARNES, } his Clerks.
CHARLES BENTON,

JOB LAYTON (Scraps), a Rag-picker.

GRACE BENTON, Abel's daughter.

RACHEL ALLEN, Matthew's sister.

BETSEY BENTON, Abel's sister.

COSTUMES.

ABEL BENTON. Blue coat, white vest, white necktie, dark pants, gray wig, side whiskers.

MATTHEW ALLEN and RICHARD CARNES. Act 1 and 2, Business suits. Act 3, Evening dress.

JOB LAYTON. Act 1, Ragged coat fastened at the waist with a rope, rough iron-gray wig, rough beard, dark pants, large boots unblacked, dark necktie, old hat. Act 2, Black pants and coat, white vest, white necktie, hair and beard trimmed. The dress should be good but slouchy.

CHARLES BENTON. Act 1, Dark pants, white shirt, a large wet

7

handkerchief thrown loosely about his neck, boots in his hand, and coat over his arm, socks on his feet, hair dripping wet. Sprinkle the clothes with bits of isinglass for a general soused appearance; change to Base Ball suit, with the letter G on breast. Act 2, Business suit. Act 3, Neat evening dress.

GRACE BENTON. Act 1, Fashionable summer dress, with shawl and hat. Act 3, White evening dress, rich and tasty.

RACHEL ALLEN. Acts 1 and 2, Neat and pretty street dress. Act 3, White.

BETSEY BENTON. Act 1, Black silk dress, scant, old-fashioned shawl and hat, gray front of hair. Act 3, Black silk dress, white bertha, front, and cap.

ACT 1. SCENE. — ABEL BENTON'S *counting-room. Desk against wall,* R. *Desk against wall,* L. *Writing table,* C., *with drawer opening at back. Chairs before desks,* R. *and* L. *Chair* R. *of table. Lounge behind table,* C. *On desks inkstands, pens, paper, &c. The entrances are from* R. *and* L. : *that on the* R. *is from the warehouse and the street; that on the* L. *leads to* ABEL BENTON'S *private room.* RICHARD CARNES *discovered seated at desk,* L.

Richard. 56 — 65 — 72 — 81 — 90. Figures, figures, figures! I'm heartily tired of this drudgery, day after day, casting up columns that add no sum total to *my* earthly happiness. If one could be as lucky as our head centre, Abel Benton, patience would indeed be a virtue. But he's one in a thousand. First a rag-picker, a searcher in cast-out heaps of rubbish for scraps of paper, rags, old junk, anything that by accumulation could produce a few pennies with which to keep soul and body together; then, by the usual stages of honest industry, rising to the more honorable position of peddler, proprietor of a small junk shop, general speculator in paper stock, and now gathering rags from every quarter of the globe, supplying almost every paper-mill in the country; with an income sufficient to glut the appetite of the most luxurious, and a name A 1 on the street; while I, with a rich and stingy old father, am forced to drudge in the counting-room of this opulent rag-picker for a meagre salary, keep myself, and grow rich on expectation. O, it's a funny world — 7 — 16 — 21 — a remarkably facetious old globe — 32 — 37 — 41. Hallo; who's there?

Enter SCRAPS, R., *with a basket. In all his scenes his eyes are roving about the stage, and in this Act he picks up scraps of rags and paper, which should be left about for that purpose.*

Scraps. Eh, hey! (*Puts his hand to his left ear with this word, always.*) O, if you please, Mr. Carnes, here's my ticket from the warehouse; twenty-five cents — white, all white, four pounds and a quarter — just twenty-five cents. Hey, Mr. Carnes.

Rich. (*takes ticket, and gives* SCRAPS *scrip from desk*). Twenty-five cents; and is that the extent of your day's pickings, Scraps?

Scraps. Hey? Yes, that's all. Pickings is hard, Mr. Carnes.

Rich. O, you'll never amass a fortune at this rate. Look at the shining example of successful rag-picking at the head of our house, and stir your stumps a little more lively, Scraps.

Scraps. Hey? Stir my stumps? O, no, can't do it. I've got the gout with too high living. Ha, ha! high living! I think I'll retire, and live on my fortune; ha, ha! my fortune! That's good; that's exceedingly good.

Rich. You're an old sinner, Scraps. Now I've no doubt you have a snug sum stowed away in one of our banks.

Scraps. Hey?

Rich. You'll cut up rich one of these days. In which of our banks do you deposit?

Scraps. Cut up pranks, at my time of life — no, no.

Rich. (*rises, crosses, looks off,* R., *then comes down* R. *of* SCRAPS). Now, look here, Scraps; you're not so deaf as you appear. I happen to want a hundred dollars. Lend it to me. I'll pay you ten per cent.; the banks only give you six. Let me have a loan —

Scraps. Hey? Let you alone? I can't hear, you know. You're on the wrong side.

Rich. (*angrily crosses to* L., *pushing* SCRAPS *back as he passes*). Bah! you old fool! None so deaf as those who won't hear. (*Sits at desk.*)

Scraps (*pointing* L.). Is Mr. Benton in there, Mr. Carnes?

Rich. Yes, he's in there, and very busy settling his last year's business. Not to be disturbed.

Scraps. O, he's a rich un, he is, and once he was as mean and dirty a rag-picker as I am. We were chummies then, we were; ha, ha! not very chummy now — not very. He was a chap what saved his money; mine went as fast as it came. He took to books; I took to billiards. He loved study; I loved sport. And so the road in which we picked parted one day; he crawled up hill, and I down. Now he's a looking off over his vast possessions from the top of the hill, and I'm picking away in the mud, far, far below. Let this be a warning to you, Mr. Carnes.

Rich. Warning to me? What do you mean?

Scraps. O, you know what I mean. You're fond of billiards, and theatres, and — the tiger — you know you are; and I know it too, for I've watched you many a night. Now Abel Benton don't like this. Here are you and Mr. Matthew Allen, equally trusted. He delights in books, you in billiards; and depend upon it both of these, like everything else about here, will be weighed on Abel Benton's scales, and, when they do, billiards will kick the beam.

Rich. You miserable street grubber, do you dare to threaten me? Leave the room at once.

Scraps. Yes, billiards is mighty captivating.

Rich. (*seizing a ruler, and approaching* Scraps, *who backs to* R.). Clear out, you croaking vagrant.

Scraps. But it takes money, Mr. Carnes, it takes money.

Rich. Fool, take that! (*Raises the ruler. Enter quickly,* R., Matthew.)

Matthew (*steps between, and arrests* Dick's *arm*). Easy, Dick, easy. Scraps' head is not thick, and the ruler is very thin. Don't spoil either.

Rich. Insolent old fool! Were I master here, he should never show his ugly face in this place. (*Goes to desk,* L.)

Mat. Then I'm very glad you're not, Dick. Scraps

is a very worthy old fellow.   Since you and I have been clerks for Mr. Benton, daily, winter and summer, he has dropped in upon us, and I, for one, should miss him.

Scraps.   Thank you, Mr. Allen.

Rich.   O, you've found your ears, have you.

Scraps.   I haven't but one, Mr. Carnes; the other's stopped, and I'm glad of it, for a poor old chap like me gets many a hard word flung at him, that can't touch the heart-strings when there's a closed door between.   I'm much obliged to you, Mr. Allen.   Mr. Carnes wanted to put me out, but, bless you, I don't mind it.   I'm never put out, never ; and mark me, *I* shan't be the one put out here — no, no.   (*Exit*, R.)

Rich.   The meddling old scamp !

Mat.   Dick, you seem out of sorts to-day.   What is the trouble between you and Scraps?

Rich.   Nothing you can mend.   Any news of the Elmyra?

Mat.   She has just been telegraphed.

Rich.   Any private signals?

Mat.   Yes, English rags, full freight, consigned to Abel Benton.

Rich.   Of course — low market, high prices, and just in the nick of time the Elmyra sails into Abel Benton's pocket with a cargo of five thousand dollars in gold. The old scrub !

Mat.   And who is old scrub ?

Rich.   The governor, the head centre, Abel Benton, of course.

Mat.   Gently, Dick, gently.   He deserves more respect.   He has been a kind master to you and me.

Rich. Well, he ought to have made money enough by this time to retire and give us a chance. Now, here's the case of the Elmyra. *You* foretold a short market; *you* proposed sending an agent across the water. Your advice was taken; it has proved a success: yours was the venture; to you should come the profits.

Mat. Dick, you are unreasonable. Listen: that ship sailing into port reminds me that seven years ago I stood on the deck of a vessel sailing into this same port. Coming to this country from old England, a lad of fourteen, leaving behind me the fresh-tufted grave of my mother, the only protector I had in the world, my only companion my sister, four years younger. Dick, you have father and mother, rich and powerful friends, everything about you comfortable and pleasant. You never knew what it is to cry with hunger, to shiver with cold, as I did in the old country; you never stood, as I stood then, on the deck of a vessel with not a cent in my pocket, knowing not what awaited me amid the domes and spires of the city we were nearing fast. If you had, Dick, if you had suffered all this, and then felt upon your shoulder the hand which fell upon mine as I leaped ashore, looked into the kindly face that I looked into, you would strain every faculty of your being to serve the interests of so kind a benefactor as Abel Benton.

Rich. Benefactor, indeed! I tell you, Matt, you think too little of yourself. Benton is shrewd. I've no doubt he read in your face, at first sight, the energy and spirit by which he has profited. You've given him hard work for every dollar expended.

Mat. Then, there's my sister. He has been like a

father to her. She is treated in his house as a daughter, every wish gratified, almost spoiled by his indulgence.

Rich. Well, he doesn't spoil us by indulgence. His old-fashioned notions put double work upon us. He won't have a safe, but requires one of us to sleep here every night. It's very lucky nothing has ever disappeared from the warehouse, for I believe he would discharge us on mere suspicion.

Mat. He's an odd man, Dick, and no one can tell to what his whims may lead; but with clear consciences, and determination to do our best, we need not fear his changing humors. (*Sits at desk*, R.)

Charley (*outside*, R.). Old rags! old rags! (*Enter*, R.) Here you are, now, a prime lot, a little damaged by salt water. Who bids? Going, going.

Mat. Why, Charley, where did you come from?

Chas. (*takes handkerchief off his neck, and wrings out the water*). The bottom of the sea. "The sea, the sea, the boundless sea." I'm a river god, a mermaid, — Charley Benton as a live mermaid; his first appearance on any stage.

Mat. Come, Charley, be sober.

Chas. Sober! Do you know where I've been? I've been in the depths of sobriety — at the bottom of the bay. I can lead you to the spot where the flounders are thickest, for I've floundered among them; where the smelts congregate, for I've smelt 'em; where the rock is in the cradle of the deep, for I went straight for it — red hot.

Rich. You've been overboard.

Chas. Considering my present humid appearance, that was not a very remarkable guess.

Mat. And you are wet through.

Chas. Thank you; that's a very dry remark. Any more interesting news?

Mat. If you don't change your clothes at once you'll be laid up for a month.

Chas. Thank you; any fool could tell me that; but don't trouble yourself; I've a dry suit in the loft.

Mat. But what sent you overboard?

Chas. My love of business. I was hurrying down the wharf to catch sight of the Elmyra, and — somebody's been shortening that wharf, for, before I knew it, I was in the briny, and bound for the bottom.

Rich. You lummux, walked overboard?

Chas. Exactly; clamoring for help, which did not arrive until I'd been down clamming at the bottom.

Mat. Well, run and change your clothes.

Chas. My base ball uniform is up stairs, and if I can keep out of the governor's way, I'm all right. Mum, boys, for he's down on the manly sport. He knows nothing of the glories of the base ball field, and if he finds me in that rig I shall catch it. (*Exit,* R.)

Rich. Clumsy chap. Served him right.

Mat. Hold on, Dick. There's the faintest shadow of a mystery here. Charley may have accidentally walked overboard, but he took precious good care to remove his boots first. Did you notice? They were as dry as mine. You'll find there is more in this than appears on the face of it.

Rich. Matt, you're always finding excuses for him.

Mat. Am I? Well, it's because he's a noble-hearted fellow. If he's not a driving business man, it's because

he has a rich father, and does not feel the need of exer-
tion. It's time Mr. Benton was informed of the arrival
of the Elmyra. Where away to-night, Dick?

Rich. The usual round : a little billiards, a peep into
the theatres, and a good time generally. Will you go
with me?

Mat. No, I thank you, Dick. It's my night on guard
here, and, besides, I don't fancy your sport. Ah, Dick,
it's a pity you're so fond of it. If Mr. Benton should get
an inkling of your predilections, 'twould go hard with you.
Have a care, old boy, have a care. (*Exit*, L.)

Rich. (*at desk*, L.). Have a care, indeed! Preach
away, parson. You fancy you are feathering your nest
by the remarkably moral life you lead. Bah ! With all
my love for sport, I can hold my place in old Benton's
warehouse. He trusts me as fully as he does you ; con-
fides to me as important business as he does to you. I
have the advantage in being the oldest, and shrewdness
enough to keep my pleasures from being noticed by the
head centre. But I'd like to see you, Matt Allen, taken
down a peg, and if ever I have the chance, you shall be
brought to your level, depend upon it. (*Writes.*)

Enter SCRAPS, *cautiously*, R.

Scraps (*aside*). I've been hunting everywhere for
Master Charley. O, he's a sly one. Hullo ! there's Mr.
Carnes again. Ho, ho ! he'd break my head, would he?
he'd turn me out, would he? We shall see. It's time
Abel Benton knew the snake he is warming. O, I'll
reward him for his kindness.

Enter CHARLEY, R., *in base ball dress. Snatches the basket from* SCRAPS, *and covers his head with it.*

Scraps. Help! murder! help! (*Extricating himself from basket.*) Hallo, Master Charley! Up to your old tricks, hey?

Chas. Tricks, indeed! I was only filling your basket with what it so much needs — old rags, old rags.

Scraps. Now — now — now — you're a funny dog, Master Charley. But, my eyes, how fine you're rigged! Going sojering, hey?

Chas. Sojering? No. This is the emblematic costume of the Gooseneck Base Ball Club. Ain't it gay, red hot.

Rich. Red hot! It will be well warmed if the governor catches you.

Chas. But I don't mean he shall. When he takes the field, " I'm out on the fly." Ah, Dick, you should join us. It's glorious sport.

Rich. Bah! it's so fatiguing and so dirty!

Chas. It may be for you, lily fingers. You'd rather spend your time in a smoky billiard room. But for me, give me the free air, the green field, strong, tough fellows striving for the mastery, every muscle alive with health, sharp eyes, eager hands, quick legs, the strike, the run, the catch. O, it's glorious! Hey, Scraps?

Scraps. O, yes. How much do you get for it?

Chas. O, pshaw, Scraps! don't be mercenary. Get fame, glory. (*Takes a small leather case from his pocket, and opens it.*) Look at that. That's what we get for it. There's a badge to be presented to Bob Dyke, our pitcher, this evening, as a slight token of the Goosenecks' appre-

2

ciation of his valuable services. And I'm to make the presentation speech. Ain't it gay?

Scraps. Well, 'tis handsome. And you to make a speech? I declare, I should like to hear you make a speech.

Chas. Would you? Then you shall. You shall be the pitcher, not exactly the figure, but you'll do for a rehearsal now. You stand there. (*Places him in* c., *and goes down,* R.) Ahem! ahem! Renowned pitcher —

Scraps. Hey?

Chas. Now what's the matter with you?

Scraps. Why, you're on the wrong side.

Chas. (*crossing to* L.). All right. I forgot the impediment. Now then. Renowned — O, stand up; present a dignified aspect.

Scraps. Hey? Me present. I thought you was a going to do that.

Chas. O, you're a muff. Stand up; throw out your chest. There, that's better. Now. Renowned pitcher! champion of the ball field, model of muscular manliness — O, hold up your head, will you?

Scraps. How can I hear if I hold up my head?

Chas. Shut up! Paragon of perfect proportions, politest of peripatetic pitchers, how much we owe thee!

Scraps. Not a cent. Mr. Carnes settled —

Chas. Shut up! As we look back to the glorious victories achieved on Potter's field, we see thy noble form animated with a spirit bold and daring —

Scraps. Hey? Spirits? 'Pon my word I never drank a drop; and as for swearing —

Chas. Shut up! In the front of battle, winning re-

nown for the Goosenecks. We would express our grati-
tude ; and it devolves upon me, the humble instrument
of our victorious nine, to present you this slight token of
our appreciation of your valuable services. Take it, prize
it for the giver's sake ; take it, wear it over your noble
heart. (*Enter*, L., MR. BENTON, *followed by* MATTHEW
ALLEN.) Take it —

Mr. Benton (*takes badge*). Thank you, and once in
my possession I shall preserve it ; depend upon that,
Charley Benton.

Chas. (*crosses to* R.). The governor. Foul ball.

Scraps. Is that all, Charley?

Mr. B. So, sir, in spite of my repeated warnings, I
find you tricked out in a garb I have forbidden, making
a fool of yourself when you should be attending to business. Shame, shame, Charles! I thought you were
more of a man.

Chas. Yes, sir, it's a mistake ; I — I — I know it's
wrong, but I tumbled overboard a while ago, and as I
was very dry — no, wet — I —

Mr. B. Tumbled overboard?

Chas. Yes, accidentally — not on purpose — walked
overboard.

Scraps. Don't you believe it, Abel Benton ; don't you
believe it. It's a lie ; a downright lie.

Chas. Scraps, I'll break your head.

Scraps. Hey? You're on the wrong side. O, I
know him, Abel Benton, I know him, the smooth-tongued
villain, and I'll expose his wickedness too.

Mr. B. Well, Job, what do you know?

Scraps. I know all about it. It's the common talk

on the wharf; and if I have but one ear; that's wide open.

Chas.   Scraps, if you say another word —

Scraps.   Hey? — O, you're on the wrong side.   O, he's a deep one.   An hour ago he was on the wharf — this scoundrel.   Walking coolly down the wharf.   Just before him was a little ragged, dirty girl —

Chas.   Scraps, Scraps, your life's in danger.

Scraps.   Hey? — You're on the wrong side.   Creeping along, picking up chips, and this rogue, this scamp, close behind her.   She reached the end of the wharf —

Chas.   Scraps, another word, and I'll strike —

Scraps.   Hey? — You're on the wrong side, I tell you. — Her foot slipped, and over she went; and this villain, this cold-blooded villain —

Mr. B.   Looked coolly on.

Scraps.   Cool, — his boots were off in a second, and over he went, seized the child, and held her head above water until they were both drawn out.   Look at him! look at the calm, cool, calculating villain.   O, he's a deep one.

Mr. B.   Charles, is this true?

Chas.   I'm sorry to say it is, sir.

Mr. B.   Sorry!   Charley, my boy, you're a noble — Hem! yes, sir, you have disobeyed my orders, and I shall see that you are punished.   As for this trinket, I'll take care of it.   (*Unlocks drawer in table*, C., *deposits the case, and then locks drawer.*)   Here it is safe, but you see it no more.   (*Exit*, L.)

Chas.   Out on the badge.   Scraps, I've a great mind to pommel you.

Mat. No you won't, Charley, for he's defeuded you. Give me your hand. You're an honor to the house.

Scraps. What did I tell you? Villany is always found out, always.

Chas. O, I'll be even with you, Scraps.

Scraps. Hey? — You're on the wrong side.

Chas. We've had quite enough of your interference; so go.

Scraps. Yes, I'll go down on the wharf, and hunt up more of your crimes. O, you're a sly one; deceive your father, hey! walk overboard, hey! Ha, ha! you'll catch it. Ha, ha! (*At door,* R.) I say, Charley, red hot, red hot! (*Exit,* R.)

Mat. Dick, here's Foley's invoice. You copy that, and I'll take Dixon's. They must both go by next mail. (*Sits at desk,* R.)

Rich. (*at desk,* L.). All right, Matt.

Chas. (*sits on table,* C.). " I saw it but a moment, but methinks I *don't* see it now." The renowned pitcher's badge has gone into the governor's drawer, and how the renowned pitcher is to get it, and how the subscriber is to present it to the renowned pitcher, are questions of vital importance, in fact, red hot. The governor won't give it up; but I must have it.

Rachel (*outside,* R.). Goodness gracious, I shall die, I know I shall.

Betsey (*outside,* R.). Do behave yourself, Rachel Allen. I declare, you mortify me to death.

Rachel. Can't go another step. (*Enters,* R., *with her arms full of bundles. She drops them in a heap on the floor,* R., *and falls on her knees.*) It's no use. It's that last camel hair shawl that broke this camel's back. Why, hallo, Charley!

Chas. And hallo, Shellie! what's the matter?

Enter AUNT BETSEY, R., *shaking her parasol at an imaginary foe outside.*

Betsey. Don't you look at me! Don't you dare to look at me! Mind your business, impudence.

Chas. What's the matter, Aunt Betsey?

Betsey. Do look at that impudent — Go away, I say. Don't stand gawking at me. S'pose he never saw a woman afore. Jest like 'em; they're all alike.

Chas. (*looking off*, R.). Why, he isn't looking at you, Aunt Betsey.

Betsey. I tell you he is. I know he is. You can't fool me.

Chas. No, he's not looking at you, for the very good reason that he's blind. It's only old Foley.

Rachel. O, Aunt Betsey! Ha, ha, ha! what blind devotion!

Betsey (*sitting in chair* R. *of table*). Well, I never! Rachel Allen, where's your dignity? Get up from that floor directly.

Chas. What's all this? Where have you been?

Rachel. Been shopping; and O, my, didn't we make a commotion! There's nothing but bare shelves and bare counters in every dry goods store from the Park to the Square.

Betsey. Goodness gracious! hear that child talk. And there's all my things a being ruined on this dirty floor.

Chas. (*picks up bundles, and places them on table*). Whose are these things?

Rachel. They're all mine, except the five largest; those are Aunt Betsey's.

Chas. And there's only six in the lot. That's a very modest way of letting me know that you've been loaded down with Aunt Betsey's purchases. Why not have them sent home?

Betsey. Young man, mind your business. When I go shopping I mean to have just what I buy, and nothing else. Them air counter chaps air dreadful spry and smilin, but they can't deceive Betsey Benton. Never!

Chas. But, Aunt Betsey, 'tis too much for Shellie's little arms.

Betsey. Young man, mind your business. When I was a gal I had to work, and I mean everybody round me shall, if I can make work for 'em.

Chas. Now look here, Aunt Betsey; you and I will have a falling out one of these days, if you don't treat Shellie better.

Betsey. Highty-tity, young man! Mind your business. She ain't a goin to be brought up to a life of idleness, I tell you.

Rachel. O, now, don't quarrel about me. Why, there's brother Matt. (*Crosses*, R., *and puts her hand on his shoulder.*) Well, brother Money Grub, how's trade?

Mat. Ah, Sunshine! The Elmyra's come. Trade is looking up.

Rachel. O, I'm so glad. I wish I was a man. It must be so grand to make money.

Chas. Why, you're avaricious, Shellie.

Rachel. No, I'm not, Charley. I want the money with which to buy richer treasures — the poor man's blessing and the sufferer's smile.

Mat. Ah, Shellie, if we could only think so after we acquire riches! But where have you been?

Rachel. Been shopping; and, don't you think, Aunt Betsey was nearly run over. O, such fun!

Betsey. Fun! fun! Well, I never! I'm most dead with fright, and that young one calls it fun!

Rachel. Yes, we were just crossing the main street, when somebody called out, " Look out, there! " And of course we looked out, and there was a running horse almost upon us. I gave one leap and landed on the sidewalk, but Aunt Betsey she just stood in the street, and flourished her parasol, when a ragged individual rushed between her and the horse, caught her up in his arms, and placed her on the sidewalk. O, she did look so funny, with her arms flying about like a windmill, and screaming like a locomotive.

Betsey. Well, I never! And you stood on the sidewalk and laughed — absolutely laughed. I never was so mortified in my life.

Rachel. Ha, ha, ha! I couldn't help it, you did look so in the arms of your preserver.

Betsey. Rachel Allen, I'm petrified! Where on airth is your dignity!

Mat. 'Twas a very serious matter. And who was the brave man who rescued you?

Betsey. How should I know? While I was looking for a dollar to give him, he slipped off.

Chas. I should think he would. A dollar for saving your life. (*Aside.*) O, it's too much.

Betsey. Where's your father?

Chas. In his office, Aunt Betsey.

Betsey. Well, Rachel, you pick up the bundles. I'll just speak to him, and then we must be getting home. (*Exit*, L.)

Rachel. Why, how queer you're dressed, Charley! Is that your working suit?

Chas. Well, no — yes, it is *one* of my working suits.

Rachel. What does the letter G stand for?

Rich. Stands for Goose, Shellie.

Rachel. Ha, ha, ha! How very appropriate!

Mat. 'Tis very appropriate, Shellie, but it doesn't stand for goose. It's the initial of Great, and, placed where it now is, it fitly represents the great heart beneath it. Charley wears that dress at this time, Shellie, because he has just saved a little girl from drowning at the risk of his own life.

Rachel. That's just like him. He's always doing something brave. (*Goes up and takes his hand.*) O, Charley, I shall love you just as long as I live.

Chas. Will you, though, Shellie? Then let me tell you that I shall ask that — I am — that you are —

Rachel. Why, what's the matter, Charley?

Chas. Well — I was going to say — that I — that I am —

Enter BETSEY, L.

Betsey. Now, Rachel, get your bundles, and we'll go.

Chas. Once for all, Aunt Betsey, I tell you I will not have it. She shall not carry those bundles.

Betsey. I say she shall. Young man, mind your business.

Chas. So I will; and it's my business to relieve the weaker sex of their cares when I can. I'll just take possession of the bundles, and bring them up to-night.

Betsey. Young man, I insist —

Chas. Now, look here, Aunt Betsey; don't get me mad; for when I get angry I always run and jump off the wharf — and I don't go alone.

Betsey. Good gracious! Do you mean to say you would throw me overboard?

Chas. I'm afraid I should if I got mad.

Betsey. Come, Rachel, let's go. That youth is on the broad road going to destruction. Come. (*Exit,* R.)

Rachel. Good by. I'm coming back with Grace when she comes for her father. O, Charley, for shame! Threatening to throw Aunt Betsey overboard! (*Exit,* R.)

Chas. Of all the aggravating creatures, Aunt Betsey is a little ahead. Why don't she get married? She's old enough. She's no earthly use in our house, except to fret and worry, and interfere in all my little arrangements. (*Enter* SCRAPS, R.) Hullo! you back again?

Scraps. Hey? yes. I've a little business with your father. I say, Master Charley, who's that lady I just met?

Chas. Lady? The young one or the old one?

Scraps. . The tall, fine-looking lady. (*Pointing,* R.) There, that one.

Chas. Fine looking! (*Aside.*) Scraps is smitten. (*Aloud.*) That's Aunt Betsey, father's sister. Did you ever see her before?

Scraps. Hey? No — yes — yes — once.

Chas. You did! Where?

Scraps. Now, now, Charley, none of that. You're on the wrong side.

Chas. (*aside*). He's smitten, red hot! By Jove, an idea. Scraps is rich. Why can't I make a match between them? Dress him up, and start him courting Aunt Betsey. That's one way to get rid of her. (*Aloud.*) Ah, Scraps, you sly dog, I thought you'd met before. She often speaks of you.

Scraps. Often speaks of me?

Chas. Yes, thinks you are not what you seem. Nobility beneath the ragged covering, soul shines through his shaggy eyebrows, and all that sort of thing. O, she's romantic.

Scraps. Often speaks of me? Well, that's singular.

Chas. Now's your chance, Scraps. Dress up; put on a bold air; you've got the money. "Woo her as the lion woos his bride;" and she'll fall into your arms.

Scraps. Yes. Well, I'll think about it; I'll think about it.

Enter MR. BENTON, L.

Mr. B. This note, Richard, must be in Captain Baxter's hands at once.

Rich. Yes, sir. I'll despatch a messenger immediately. (*Exit,* R.)

Mr. B. Matthew, the Spooner Mills are short of stock. We can get our own price for the Elmyra's cargo.

Mat. Then I'd better run up in the morning.

Mr. B. I think you had. Take the first train. You

can return in the evening. By the way, who sleeps here
to-night?

Mat. 'Tis my watch, sir.

Mr. B. That's bad. You cannot catch the early
train.

Mat. O, yes, if Charley can come down at six.

Mr. B. No ; I'll relieve you myself.

Mat. All right, sir ; I'll make my arrangements ac
cordingly. (*Exit*, R.)

Mr. B. Charles, go into my office. I've a few words
for you.

Chas. Yes, sir. (*Aside.*) Words that burn — red
hot ! (*Exit*, L.)

Mr. B. ·Well, Job, old friend, how wags the world
with you?

Scraps. Hey? O, well, Abel; well. I pick up
enough to keep soul and body together, and now and then
a dollar for a rainy day.

Mr. B. Why will you persist in this vagabond life?
You would be a valuable man to me in the warehouse.
I have often urged you to take a place here.

Scraps. I know it, Abel ; but I like to be my own
master. Here I should be cramped. Regular hours and
regular work — Not for me, Abel ; not for me.

Mr. B. I don't like to see an old friend creeping
about the streets, picking rags from the gutter like a
vagrant. Look at me. The old life is almost blotted
out of memory. I have made my way to a respectable
position, while you, who started in life with me, still
cling to the old existence. It's too bad, Job.

Scraps. No, Abel, not too bad, for it's the life I love.

You were ambitious to rise in the world ; to get money. You have been successful, and your old friend rejoices in your prosperity. But all your wealth requires much care. You are anxious, uneasy. There are hard lines in your face. The failure of one of your speculations would go near to break your heart. While I manage to scrape, " here a little, and there a little," roam about, look and laugh at the follies of the world, watch the struggles and triumphs of busy men, and speculate, without risk, on the rise and fall of stocks.

Mr. B. That's very ragged philosophy, Job.

Scraps. Hey? Philosophy? No, that's freedom, and freedom gives one so much time for observation to acquire knowledge. Why, Abel, I know more about your business than you do. With all your wealth, you are at the mercy of your clerks.

Mr. B. My clerks are models of industry, energy, and honesty.

Scraps. All of them?

Mr. B. Yes ; I would not have in my employ one hour a young man whom I could not trust fully.

Scraps. Blind, Abel, blind. I know better. I've seen one of your clerks at the gaming-table night after night. I have seen him enter places where no honest man should go. I have seen this, Abel. I'm a little dull of ear, but I've a sharp eye.

Mr. B. One of my clerks, Job? Which one?

Scraps. Hey? — Now, you're on the wrong side. Abel Benton, find out yourself. I will watch, but you must trap the game.

Mr. B. Is it my son? I tremble while I ask it.

Scraps. What, Charley? No, no; he's the soul of honor.

Mr. B. Is it —

Scraps. No, no; fair play, Abel. I've set you on the track. I shall do no more.

Mr. B. Very well, I will watch, and if I have the faintest suspicion I will act. My clerks! Job, if I did not know you so well, I should doubt you, and not them.

Scraps. O, I'm all right. Now for a little business. I had a scare last night, Abel. Somebody broke into my room, seized me by the throat, and demanded money; but I had strength enough to throw him off, and rouse my neighbors. He escaped; my money was safe; but it must be put in a safer place. (*Produces small bag.*) Here is a hundred dollars, all in gold. You, Abel, must take care of it.

Mr. B. Certainly. (*Takes bag, goes to table, c., sits and writes.*) I shall not count it; your word is enough. It shall be well taken care of. Here's your receipt. (*Gives receipt.*) The money shall go in here. (*Opens the drawer in table where he has placed the badge, and locks it.*)

Scraps. What! Leave my money there after what I told you?

Mr. B. For that very reason. You have directed suspicion to one of my clerks. Your money should be the bait to catch the rogue. Hush! No more. Here is my daughter.

Enter GRACE, R.

Grace (c.). Good afternoon, father. Are you ready to escort me home?

Mr. B. (L.). In a few moments, Grace. This is an old friend of mine, Job Layton.

Grace. One I have longed to see. (*Crosses to* SCRAPS, R., *and takes his hand.* — SCRAPS *confused.*) My father often speaks of you, his old friend. Why don't you come and see us? You shall be heartily welcome, and I will do my best to entertain you.

Scraps. Lord bless you, pretty one, your father and I parted company years ago — he to go up, I to stick in the mud. I go to your house? Why, your servants would slam the door in my face.

Grace. No, no, Mr. Layton, nobody is driven from our door. There's an easy-chair waiting for you, and if you will come you shall find yourself with true friends. Now promise me you will come.

Scraps. Yes, yes, some time I will come. (*Turns to door,* R.) Good by. (*Aside.*) She's a darling. Ah, Abel may well be proud of such a daughter. And I, — I might have had a daughter to hang about my neck, to brighten my home, instead of being a lonely, ragged scavenger. O, Job, Job, I begin to doubt you. Freedom is all very well, but the chain which a loving child throws about a father makes slavery worth enduring. Bah, Job! You a philosopher! More likely an old fool — an old fool. (*Exit,* R.)

Mr. B. Grace, if that man survives me, look to it that he never suffers. When I was poor he was my best friend. Many a time in our rag-picking days he has robbed his basket to fill mine. Under that old coat there's a true heart. He must never suffer.

Grace. Never, if I can help it, father. Charley is very fond of him. Where is Charley, father?

Mr. B. In disgrace. Waiting in my room for the lecture he so richly deserves.

Grace. Why, what has he been doing?

Mr. B. Jumping overboard to save a drowning child. I could forgive that, but he's rigged himself in that outlawed sporting suit, for which he shall be well lectured.

Enter DICK, R.

Rich. Good afternoon, Miss Benton. (*Bows, and crosses to desk, L.)*

Grace. Good afternoon, Mr. Carnes.

Enter MATTHEW, R.

Mat. Ah, Miss Grace! You are early.

Grace. Matthew, I'm glad to meet you. (*Shakes hands with him.)* Yes, I've come to carry father off.

Enter RACHEL, R.

Rachel. There, I've torn my dress with one of those dirty bales. I declare, I can't see the use of having so many rags about.

Mr. B. To turn into money, Shellie.

Rachel. Hallo, Uncle Abe! Out of your den? Come, get your hat. We've come to lead you home.

Mr. B. I'll be ready soon. By the by, young gentlemen, I have placed a hundred dollars in gold in the upper drawer of that table for safe keeping. It belongs to Job Layton.

Mat. A hundred dollars? Isn't that an unsafe place for so large a sum?

Mr. B. Not while I have honest clerks. I shall be

very glad to see you at my home to-morrow evening. You will return in ample time, Matthew. You will meet there my partner.

All. Your partner!

Mr. B. Yes, I am getting old, and have decided to take a partner — a young and active man. You will have an opportunity to make his acquaintance before he enters upon his duties. (*Exit,* L.)

Grace. Now he's going to scold Charley. But not if I can help it. I've prevented it before, and I'll try it again. (*Exit,* L.)

Mat. (*sits at his desk*). A partner! A young and active man! Who can it be?

Rachel (*comes down and leans over his chair*). What's the matter, brother?

Mat. Thinking, Sunshine, thinking. We must all do that, you know.

Rachel. Well, then, tell me your thoughts. My brother should have no secrets from his keeper. That's the bargain, Matthew.

Mat. A new master is to step in here, Shellie — here, where, for seven years, we have worked so well together — the old master and his clerks. A man with new ideas, perhaps tyrannical, to upset the old smooth order of things. What says my keeper to that?

Rachel. She says, Think on, brother. Think of the good old man who laid his hand on your shoulder so kindly when you were a stranger in a strange land; who has been your steadfast friend from that hour to this, and say, Let new masters come; while the old master lives I have faith that he will never desert me.

3

Mat. Right, my keeper, right. Do what he may. I will believe he loves and trusts me.

Enter CHARLEY, .L.

Chas. Well, I'm out on that. After roosting on a high stool for nearly half an hour, anxiously expecting a storm, that dear sister of mine drops in just as the clouds begin to gather, and all's sunshine. Hallo, Shellie! You here again?

Rachel. Yes, Charley. Come, pick up the bundles, and start the caravan.

Chas. But we must wait for Grace.

Rachel. Then let's take a stroll down the wharf. I want to see the place where you walked overboard.

Chas. Yes, where I put my foot in it. I can lead you to it. It's a delightful spot, so cool and retired. Come along. (*Exeunt Chas. and Rachel,* R.)

Rich. Well, Matt.

Mat. Well, Dick.

Rich. What are you going to do about it — the new partner?

Mat. Accept the new order of things, and work as diligently as ever.

Rich. Matt Allen, you're a fool! There should be no partner in this concern except you or me. The head centre cannot want capital. Perhaps this is a surprise for one of us.

Mat. Surprise? That's not his way of doing business, Dick. Think of our staid, sober old master perpetrating a joke! I couldn't imagine it. No, it's an outsider, —who, I cannot guess.

Rich. I have a strong suspicion, Mat, that you are the man. You have a strong friend beside the throne.

Mat. A strong friend? Who do you mean?

Rich. Grace Benton. It needs no very sharp eyes to see that she looks upon you with favor. Always a smile, a pleasant word, for *you.* She listens as though you were an oracle when you speak, and blushes when your step is heard. All sure signs. Don't be a fool, Mat. She's a rich catch. Be bold, and she is yours.

Mat. (*rising, indignantly*). Silence, Dick Carnes! Another word and I shall forget that we are friends, and chastise you for your insolence. Do you think me so base as to take advantage of the kindness that seeks to make me forget my humble position? so mean as to betray the trust reposed in me by my employer? Grace Benton is too high in social position for me to dare approach her as a suppliant for her hand or heart. Dick, I believe I am an honest man. I look upon a fortune-hunter as no better than a thief snatching at the treasures of another; and rather than have this imputation cast at me I'd leave this place forever.

Rich. But, Mat, if she loves —

Mat. Silence! Another word and we are enemies. (*Sits,* R.)

Rich. (*aside*). High and mighty! Chastise me for my insolence! Well, two can play at that game. An honest man, indeed! He's too honest. He has no suspicion that the new partner is himself. I have. And he's to step above me. I'd like to thwart the head centre. If he could be made to suspect Mat! But how?

Ah, the drawer! Scraps's hundred dollars! The head centre has the key, but it's not the only key that opens. The key of Mat's desk fits that lock. I know, for I've tried it. It's his watch to-night. I've an idea. (*Rises, puts on his hat, and crosses,* R.) Mat, don't get angry. You deserve the partnership, and you deserve the girl. It's a pity you can't have both. Good night.—(*Aside, at door,* R.) An honest man! I've known a fortune to be lost in a single night, and why not a character. Mat Allen, this night I'll play for yours. (*Exit,* R.)

Mat. She looks upon me with favor. She, the bright being that I have worshipped afar off, as men look upon treasures far beyond their reach. What could he mean? Have I betrayed myself? Does he know how madly I love her? No, no; never by word, look, or act have I betrayed my secret. Ah, Grace, Grace! glorious, unattainable; the idol of a cultivated circle, with a throng of admirers about you, your fortune is a safeguard against the approach of the humble worshipper — (GRACE *enters, advances across stage, and leans on his chair, listening*) — who would die to show his devotion. Year by year this love has grown upon me, and now 'tis almost too strong to prison in my heart. But I will be strong. I know 'tis an honest love, that could boldly speak were all the barriers of wealth and station removed. But this can never be; so to my heart alone, as to a sacred shrine, I'll go to worship you, my glorious Grace.

Grace. Dreaming the happy hours away, Matthew?

Mat. (*rises in confusion*). What — Grace — why — how — what — I beg your pardon. Did you speak?

Grace. Why, bless me, Matthew, what's the matter?

Have I interrupted some desperate plot, or some dream of love? You really look frightened.

Mat. Do I? Well, it's very natural. — No, I don't mean that. Does your father want me?

Grace. No; but I do. Now, compose yourself, and we will talk business. Do you know what day to-morrow is?

Mat. Why, it's Wednesday — isn't it?

Grace. Isn't it! What a bright business man. To-morrow is the anniversary of a very important event.

Mat. Your birthday?

Grace. O, that's not important. To-morrow is the anniversary of the entrance of Matthew Allen into business life.

Mat. And you remember this?

Grace. Indeed I do, for 'twas the beginning of a very happy life for all of us. 'Twas then I formed a dear friendship, which has continued until this day.

Mat. Ah, Grace, it is so kind of you to say it, — you, who are so exalted in society, to confess friendship for a poor man.

Grace. Poor man! I confess no such thing. The friendship, I admit, is with a brave fellow, who has battled night and day to serve the man who once befriended him; rich in honest worth, noble in every manly accomplishment; a man with a strong arm and a quick brain, who has the right to seek and claim the highest station, or woo and win the highest lady in the land.

Mat. Grace, Grace! This to me?

Grace. To you, Matthew, for you are the man. To-morrow my father makes choice of a partner. Who it is

I do not know. He has kept his secret even from me. I know not what changes may be made, but you, Matthew, must leave this place.

Mat. I leave this place? You know not what you say. I cannot do it.

Grace. Not do it? Why not?

Mat. Because I love you, Grace. I have hidden it so deep that I thought 'twould never escape me. But I must speak. I love you, Grace, dearly, madly, I know. Let me stay here. I will still be diligent in business. I care not who may come to lord it here; only let me be near you.

Grace. No, Matthew, you must go. Do you think I will allow you, my friend, to be supplanted in this place by a stranger. No, Matthew, you have energy and talent. Build for yourself. Imitate the example of your master, and take a partner.

Mat. A partner, Grace? You know not what you say. Where could I find a partner with capital, for that is what I should need?

Grace. O, I'll find one for you, never fear; one who will join you in any enterprise — strong, brave, true.

Mat. Where will you find me such a partner?

Grace. Here, Matthew, here, with a capital of earnest, true love. I will be your partner.

Mat. Am I dreaming? You, Grace, you?

Grace. Yes, I; the woman you have loved so long. Ah, Matthew! we cannot hide it. Try all we may, it speaks in the flush of the cheek, the gleam of the eye, the trembling speech. You have told me that you loved me, and I — I — Well, I am your partner, you know, Matthew.

Mat. Dear, dear Grace! My partner for life?

Grace. For life, Matthew.

Mat. Then on this hand —

Grace. No, no, Matthew. The head of the new house should have higher·aspirations.

Mat. Grace, you're an angel! (*Puts his arm about her waist, and kisses her lips. — Enter, L., BENTON, with his hat and cane; R., CHARLEY and RACHEL. — GRACE and MATTHEW separate, look down, confused.*)

Mr. B. (*aside*). So, so; signed, sealed, and delivered. Good, good.

Rachel. It's a match, Charley. Did you hear that smack?

Chas. Do you think I'm deaf. 'Twas red hot, Shellie, red hot!

CURTAIN.

ACT 2. SCENE. — *Same as in Act* 1. *Dark. Candle burning on table,* C. MATTHEW *seated at* L. *of it, his hand on* RACHEL'S *shoulder. She sits on a box at his feet, her arm resting upon his knee.*

Mat. And so, Shellie, you have stolen away from your cheerful home, with me to keep vigil in this gloomy place.

Rachel. Yes, brother. Uncle Abe was busy at his books, Charley had gone out, and Aunt Betsey was nodding over her knitting, so I just put on my hat and shawl, scampered off, and here I am, to spend an hour with you.

Mat. Ever thoughtful, Sunshine. You well knew your bright face would light up the old counting-room, as it has every dark scene in my life. Ah, sister mine, how dreary the last seven years would have been without you to comfort and console.

Rachel. Seven years! Why so it is, and to-morrow, to-morrow is the day we celebrate. I declare, I'd almost forgotten it. It seems but yesterday that we stood beside the death-bed of our mother. Poor mother! how she must rejoice at our prosperity, for I feel her presence always.

Mat. Yes, sister; ever near us. Dark was the life journey of the best of mothers. Heaven guard us from thought or act that might disturb her peace or sully the brightness of her pure spirit.

Rachel. Amen to that, brother. Dear mother! Can I ever forget her last night upon earth. I was alone with her. She called me to her. The light fast fading from her eyes, her face white as the pillow on which she rested, her thin, white hand feebly sought to grasp mine; but still the sweet, patient smile was there. "Shellie," she said, — dear, dear mother! — "I am going — going to sleep. No more toil, no more trouble for me. 'Twill be a long, refreshing sleep. I must not repine, yet 'tis hard to leave you to battle with the world. And the other, — my boy, your brother, — O, Shellie, temptations will be around him. He must work for you both. Let him always feel the sunshine of a sister's love. Be his helper, his counsellor, his keeper. . Sacrifice the dearest wish of your heart, if you can save him from the cold world's cruel snares." — Dear, dear mother! (*Weeps.*)

Mat. Nay, nay, sister, do not weep. She is an angel now. Nobly have you fulfilled her last request. Ever near me, ever thoughtful of my comfort, ever consoler of my dark hours, how much I owe to you. Ah, Sunshine, 'tis the strong arm that clears the path, but 'tis the gentle hand that points the way, revives the failing strength, and heals the stinging wounds. You have indeed been my keeper. Now dry your eyes, for I want your advice. You know we are to have no secrets from each other.

Rachel. That's the compact. Have you a secret?

Mat. Yes, indeed; an important one. I'm in love.

Rachel. O, that's no secret.

Mat. Indeed, sharp eyes! Well, I've another, then. I'm engaged. Wish me joy, sister. Grace Benton, the rich, beautiful, charming Grace Benton, has promised to be my wife.

Rachel. Well, I declare! And I suppose you want my consent.

Mat. Your consent?

Rachel. Certainly, sir. Am I not your guardian? Very well, sir; you shall have it. Bring her to me, and I will place my hand on your heads, and " bless you, my children," in the most approved manner. O, I'm so glad! But, stop! she has a father.

Mat. I am aware of that. Now what shall I do? Go to him, confess my love, and ask his consent, or run away with her?

Rachel. Both, of course — that is, one at a time. Ask his consent. If he declines the honor of an alliance, elope. (*Knock outside,* R.) Good gracious! What's that?.

Mat. It sounded very much like a knock. Perhaps a message ; perhaps some one for you. (*Knock repeated.*) At any rate, I'll soon find out. (*Rises ; takes the candle.*) Keep quiet, Sunshine. I'll be back in a minute. (*Exit,* R.)

Rachel (*sits in chair* L. *of table*). No secrets from each other, and I haven't told him mine. Come here on purpose too. For I'm in love — engaged. Charley Benton has promised to be my wife — no, my husband. Shall I ask his father's consent, or run away with him. Dear Charley ! he's such a queer fellow. I wonder if a young lady ever had a proposal from a man with his arms full of dry goods before. It all happened as we were going home to-night. " Shellie," said he, " dear Shellie !" And then he squeezed my arm, and dropped a bundle. " Plague take these bundles. — Shellie, I love you !" Another squeeze, and away went another bundle. I thought I should have died with laughter.

Enter MATTHEW, R.

Mat. (*places candle on table*). A note for me, Shellie.

Rachel. A note? From whom?

Mat. That's just what I'm going to find out. (*Opens note.*) Hallo ! from Charley !

Rachel. From Charley Benton?

Mat. Yes. (*Reads.*) " Dear Mat : I'm in trouble. If you don't want me locked up for the night, come to Murphy's billiard-hall and rescue the subscriber, Charley Benton." What does this mean?

Rachel. Charley in trouble? O, Mat, go at once !

Mat. I cannot, Shellie. 'Twould cost me my situation. I am placed here in trust. Mr. Benton would never forgive me should I desert my post. Foolish fellow! he's always getting into a scrape.

Rachel. You must get him out of this. Think, Mat, 'tis his own son. He must not be locked up.

Mat. I dare not go, Shellie. To leave this place would be ruin to me.

Rachel. To be locked up in a cell would be ruin to him. Think of the disgrace. O, for my sake, brother, do go.

Mat. Your sake, Shellie?

Rachel. Yes, mine. I am his promised wife.

Mat. Shellie! And you have kept this from me?

Rachel. I came here to-night to tell you; but your happiness, of course, took precedence, and I must wait to tell mine. You will save him — won't you, Mat?

Mat. But there's no one to leave here.

Rachel. Yes, I am here, and you know I'm a famous keeper. I'll guard everything while you're away. Now go, that's a good brother. Here's your hat. (*Gives him hat.*)

Mat. Well, I'll go, Shellie, for your sake. I don't like to leave you here alone. Keep quiet, and do not leave the room. (*Exit, R.*)

Rachel (*sits L. of table. Speaks slowly*). Charley in trouble! Won't I pull his ears for him! What can he have done? Nothing wrong. — He's such a rash fellow! — What's that? How lonesome it is here! What can I do to amuse myself? (*Takes book from table.*) "Promissory Notes," — that's not very promising reading. (*Takes up another.*) "Bills Payable," — O, that won't pay. What's that? There's somebody at the door. I hear a

key in the lock. Can Mat have returned so soon?
Hark! Steps! and coming this way! 'Tis not his
tread; 'tis stealthy, creeping! What shall I do? It
may be a burglar. O, heavens! I'll blow out the light.
(*Blows out light.*) Who can it be? O, I wish Mat
was here! What will become of me? I'm shivering
with fear. Let me hide somewhere. (*Crouches at end of
lounge,* L.) Nearer, nearer! I can hear my heart beat.

Enter RICHARD, *stealthily,* R.

Rich. So, so! I've tricked the faithful watchman.
The bait took, and he's off on a bootless errand. Well
planned, my boy. Now for the key. (*Creeps to desk,* R.)

Rachel. Somebody's creeping about the room!
Heaven protect me!

Rich. (*takes key from lock*). All right. Now for the
gold. (*Passes to table,* C.) Here's the drawer. The
key fits. Open sesame! (*Opens drawer.*) Here's
Scraps' shiners. (*Takes out bag, locks drawer, creeps
back to desk,* R., *and places key as before.*) Successful
burglary! The gold is in my possession. Mat Allen
will be suspected, and the partnership blown sky high for
the present. (*At door,* R.) I must be off. He'll see
the trick, and be back — but too late, too late! The
treasure's flown. (*Exit,* R.)

Rachel (*comes forward*). Gone! 'Twas a burglar.
The drawer has been robbed, — robbed in Mat's absence,
— and I, who should have protected it with my life,
skulked in a corner like a coward. What shall I do?
O, brother, did I counsel you wrong? I'll pursue him
until help appears, then have him secured. Yes, 'tis the

only course left. (*Creeps to door*, R.) Hark! Gracious heavens, he is returning for more booty! Shall I raise an alarm? No, no; who could hear me? 'Twould be but the signal for my own destruction. O, Mat, Mat, why don't you come? (*Creeps back to hiding-place*, L.)

Enter CHARLEY, R., *with arms outstretched.* *Walks against table*, C.

Chas. O, crackee! (*Creeps down*, R. *Walks against desk*, R.) O, Gemini! Well, this is a hard road to travel! I never could have believed it, never. Our Mat deserting his post — for it must have been him I saw leaving the warehouse. Now where can he have gone? It's very lucky I had my key, or my little plot to secure the pitcher's badge would have been a dead failure. Ah, ha, my good father, I do hate to thwart your plans, but what's a fellow to do that has to present a badge, and has no badge to present? So I'm going to avail myself of your key, which I quite accidentally found in your pocket, to open your drawer and secure the badge. I wish Mat was here, for I could very easily have defended my action; but this looks very like burglary. However, the renowned pitcher must not be disappointed. So here goes. (*Goes to table*, C., *unlocks drawer, takes out badge, locks drawer.*) There you are, my beauty, to make glad the heart of Bob Dyke. Now for the Goosenecks. (*Crosses to* R. *of table.*) Might as well have a smoke as I go down. (*Puts cigar in his mouth.*) Wonder if I can find a match. (*Searches pockets.*)

Rachel. What is he doing now? O, if I could but

secure the villain ! If I could but get a look at his face,
that I might know him again ! (*Creeps up to table, back*
L. *corner, leans forward anxiously.*)

Chas. I've found one. (*Draws match across table.*)

Rachel. Ah, he strikes a light. Courage, Shellie,
courage.

Chas. All right. (*When the match is well lighted,
brings it up to his cigar. It illumines his face.*)

Rachel. Gracious heavens ! Charley Benton ! (*Falls
on lounge.*)

Chas. What's that? Rats ! rats ! (*Flings book,* L.)
" Dead for a ducat."

QUICK CURTAIN.

ACT 3. SCENE. — *Parlor in* ABEL BENTON'S *house.*
Lounge, L. H. *corner. Table,* C., *back. Arm-chair on
rollers* R. *of table. Arm-chair on rollers,* R. C. *Chair
against wall, near* R. *entrance.* RACHEL *discovered
lying on lounge with her face buried in her handkerchief.*

Rachel (*raising her head and throwing her handkerchief
across the room*). There, I'm just going to put an end
to this business. All day long I've been lying round,
making myself wretched, and crying until my eyes ache
for a miserable — I was just going to say thief. Well,
he is a thief. He robbed his father's drawer, that's certain. I saw him myself. Charley Benton — my Charley ! — O, dear ! where's my handkerchief? No, I won't

drop another tear. He isn't worth it. And I, like a little fool, instead of telling Mat all about it, must needs lie to shield him. I hadn't the heart to tell my brother, when he asked me if anything had happened, — for he hadn't found Charley, — that Charley had been there. My Charley! — Where's my handkerchief? No, I won't cry. I will keep his secret, but I won't shed another tear. I wonder what he took. Uncle Abe is awful sober, but he says nothing about a robbery, and Charley — I've taken precious good care to keep out of his way — I'll have nothing to say to him. It's most time for Mat to be back. I dread the meeting. How can I look him in the face after deceiving him so?

Enter CHARLEY, R.

Chas. Ah, Shellie, I've caught you at last. Now, you coquettish puss, explain the meaning of this avoidance of me for a whole day.

Rachel (*rising*). Mr. Benton.

Chas. Hallo! That's not my name. It's plain Charley.

Rachel. Then, plain Charley, you will oblige me by keeping your distance, by calling me Miss Allen, and by avoiding me, as I shall endeavor to avoid you, in future.

Chas. Why, Shellie, what's the matter? Last night you told me that you loved me.

Rachel. Last night I thought you worthy of any woman's love. I have found out my mistake.

Chas. But, Shellie, I am all in the dark.

Rachel. I was; but a ray of light, just the gleam of a match, has wonderfully dispelled the darkness in which

I was enveloped. . You understand — a match. Henceforth we are strangers. (*Exit*, L.)

Chas. A match. It's the worst match ever I took a hand in. What does she mean? Does she mean the match we made last night? Is she going to throw it off without a trial? I don't like this, for I love her dearly. For her sake, last night, after the presentation, I withdrew from the Gooseneck Nine. I must know the cause of this sudden change. It's some of Aunt Betsey's work, perhaps. But I'll know. She's too dear a girl to give up without a struggle.

Enter SCRAPS, R., *in full evening dress, with his basket under his arm.*

Scraps. Here I am, Charley, in full regimentals.

Chas. Scraps, old fellow! — I beg your pardon, — Job Layton, Esq. Well, well, it's astonishing what good clothes can accomplish. But you don't want that basket.

Scraps. Hey?

Chas. You don't want that basket. It's out of place.

Scraps. Well, I don't know about that. There's nothing like having an eye to business. (*Picks up* RACHEL's *handkerchief, and puts it in the basket.*)

Chas. Put it in the hall. Sink the shop here.

Scraps. Just as you say. (*Exit*, R.)

Chas. He's a splendid old chap. Now if we could only make Aunt Betsey believe so! He's just the man to make her a good husband. I think if we could take her by surprise she might accept Scraps, for I don't believe she ever had an offer. There's nothing like being quick in these matters; so I'll bring them together at once.

Enter SCRAPS, R.

Scraps. There, I've put it up stairs with my old togs. Now, what next?

Chas. Scraps, you have often said that any favor I might ask of you would be freely granted.

Scraps. To be sure I have; and I say it again.

Chas. All right. Then I ask you to marry.

Scraps. Hey? You're on the wrong side.

Chas. You're on the wrong side of matrimony, and the sooner you change your position the better. I've found a wife for you. Follow my instructions and you will be a happy man.

Scraps. Marry! I? O, come, Charley, none of your jokes. Who'd marry me — an old rag-picker?

Chas. A poor old rag-picker — with forty thousand dollars.

Scraps. Hush! Do you want to ruin me?

Chas. I know where you deposit.

Scraps. Well, don't tell all you know. Who's the lady?

Chas. Aunt Betsey, the lady you saw at the office. O, Scraps, you'd make a splendid uncle.

Scraps. O, but this is all nonsense. She doesn't know me; I've never met her; we're total strangers; it's absurd, ridiculous. I'm going home.

Chas. No, you're not; you're going to meet Aunt Betsey to-night; and take my advice, Scraps, propose at once. There's nothing pleases a woman so well as an energetic lover.

4

Scraps. But, Charley, I don't know how.

Chas. It's easy enough. Tell her you've long admired her; you have heard of her sweet disposition, her amiable qualities.

Scraps. But I can't, Charley. I should be sure to make a mess of it.

Chas. O, it's easy enough. Here's the programme: I introduce you — " Miss Benton, Mr. Layton, a gentleman who has called on particular business." I leave you alone. You bow; offer her a chair; take one yourself. A short pause. You speak. " Madam, 'tis a beautiful evening." She answers, " Delightful, sir." Then you, with a sigh, — don't forget that, — " But this trait of Nature is not confined to the weather alone. *Some* women " — emphasize the *some* — " resemble it." She sighs, blushes, and says, " Ah me." You speak quick. " You have unconsciously spoken my thoughts. 'Tis you, indeed," — clasp your hands, — " on whom my thoughts are fixed. Why have you so long remained single? Your attractive appearance, your graceful carriage, your classic face, your coal-black hair — "

Scraps. Hold on, Charley. That's too much. The beautiful evening, and ah me, and the sighs, are all very well, but the carriages, the coals, and all that, are too much.

Chas. O, these are merely complimentary epithets. You can number them: one, attractive appearance; two, graceful carriage; three, classic face; four, coal-black hair; five, amiable temper.

Scraps (counting his fingers). One, attractive appearance; two, graceful carriage, — all right, I'll keep tally on my fingers. What next?

Chas. The rest you must leave to inspiration, for here she comes. Tell her you adore her, and throw yourself on your knees, beg her to bestow her hand — Here she is.

Scraps. But, Charley, I shall make a mess, I know I shall.

Enter BETSEY, R.

Betsey. Well, I never. There's that front door standing wide open, and the coal bin just as full as it can be, too, and Abel away at this time of night, and Mr. Johnson standin in his front yard a smokin a nasty pipe. If there's anything I detest, it's a pipe. When Abel had them gas pipes put in, I told him jest how it would be, though what that's got to do with smokin tobacco the Lord only knows. Why, here's Charley, and a strange man, too. Wonder if he wiped his feet.

Chas. Good evening, Aunt Betsey. This is my friend, my *wealthy* friend. Miss Benton, Mr. Job Layton.

Betsey. How do you do, Mr. Job Layton? 'Pears to me I've heard one of them names afore. Layton! Why, bless me, there was a family of Laytons lived right opposite us — poor as puddock, too. Any relation of that tribe?

Chas. O, no; Mr. Layton is descended from a very aristocratic family, of very ancient origin.

Betsey. Biblical, pr'aps. There was a Layton in my family Bible. — No, 'twan't, nuther; 'twas Job, the man who had so many blisters. Pr'aps he was one of your family.

Chas. Aunt Betsey, Mr. Layton has a very delicate

matter to bring to your attention. He wishes to consult
you on a subject that lies near his heart.

Betsey. What's the matter with him? Hope 'tain't
neurology or rheumatics. That's always fatal when it
affects the heart. What's his symptoms?

Chas. I'll leave him to explain. Treat him kindly,
for he is one of the best of men.

Betsey. Is he? Well, so are they all, till they're
found out. There was Judith Higborn's husband. Why,
folks thought butter wouldn't melt in his mouth, he was
so meek, till Judith sent him one day to the milliner for
her bunnet, and that was the last ever seen of the husband, or the milliner, or the bunnet. Spring bunnet, too,
wuth ten dollars.

Chas. Well, listen to his complaint, and remember
he has my recommendation as an excellent husband.
(*Exit,* R.)

Betsey (*aside*). Husband? Whose, I wonder? He
don't look very bright. Well, Mr. Layton, what's your
symptoms? (SCRAPS *bows, wheels chair down from* C.,
and bows, motioning BETSEY *to be seated.*) Thank you.
(*Sits.*) Well, he's perlite, anyhow. (SCRAPS *goes to* R.,
wheels down chair R. *of* BETSEY.) What a draft from
that door! Guess I'll take the other chair. (*Moves into
chair placed by* SCRAPS.)

Scraps. Hey? She's on the wrong side. That won't
do. I can't hear a word. (*Passes behind* BETSEY, *takes
the chair at her* L., *and wheels it round to her* R.)

Betsey. Law sakes, you needn't have troubled yourself. (*Moves to the other chair.*) That was just as comfortable, just as comfortable.

Scraps (*looking at her*). It's no use. I can't hear a word there. (*Is about to move the vacant chair, as before.*)

Betsey. What ails the man? Stop! stop! Sit down. (SCRAPS *looks at her, then sits.*) Something the matter with his heart? I should think 'twas his head. Now, then, what's the symptoms?

Scraps. I can't hear a word. (*A short pause. — They look at each other.*) Madam, it's a delightful evening.

Betsey. Delightful evening! The man's a lunatic: I know it. Why, it's raining cats and dogs. The mud is twelve inches deep. It's horrid, horrid!

Scraps (*aside*). Don't hear a word. (*Aloud.*) But this freak of nature is not confined to the weather alone; *some* women are just like it.

Betsey. Now, what does he mean by that? *Some* women are horrid! Does he mean me?

Scraps (*aside*). She spoke, but I heard nothing. (*Aloud.*) Yes, you have unconsciously spoken my thought. 'Tis you, indeed.

Betsey. What? O, the man's a lunatic; he certainly is. He ought to be put in a strait thimajig at once.

Scraps (*aside*). What comes next? Single, single. (*Aloud.*) No wonder you have remained single so long.

Betsey. The sarcastic wretch.

Scraps (*aside*). So far, so good. Now then. (*Counts his fingers.*) One, appearance — (*Aloud.*) Your venerable appearance —

Betsey. O, the wretch ! And he old enough to be my father.

Scraps (counts his fingers. — Aside). Two, form — *(Aloud.)* Your *antique* form —

Betsey. O, I'd like :o strangle him !

Scraps (counting. — Aside). Three, face — *(Aloud.)* Your coal-black face—

Betsey. O, Charley Benton, you shall pay for this.

Scraps (counting. — Aside). Four, hair — *(Aloud.)* Your more antique hair —

Betsey. The man's a fool.

Scraps (counting. — Aside). Five, temper — *(Aloud.)* Your versatile temper —

Betsey. Stop, stop, I say ! You've said quite enough. *(Rises.)*

Scraps. Hey? *(Aside.)* What next? *(Aloud.)* You are dying for me, or I am for you, it don't make much difference. *(Falls on his knees.)* Behold me at your feet. Bestow upon me your hand. — " If ever I cease to love — "

Betsey. I will ; there. *(Boxes his ears, first right, then left.)* There ! You're a fool, or a lunatic. If you ever show your face here again I'll scratch your eyes out, you mean, contemptible old ragamuffin. You jest make yourself scarce, or I'll have the police after you. Come here again, and I'll have a boiler of hot water ready, and use it, too. Venerable, indeed ! You old idiot ! *(Exit, R.)*

Scraps. Evidently not a success. Well, I'm glad of it. I've made a fool of myself to please the boy. I don't know what she said, but I'm on the wrong side. *(Rises.)*

Enter MR. BENTON, R.

Mr. B. Ah, Job, you're the very man I wanted. But how's this? Here in my house, and dressed so fine! What is the meaning of this?

Scraps. O, it's one of Charley's jokes. He wanted to bring me out in society. (*Aside.*) And he has, with a vengeance.

Mr. B. Well, I'm glad to see you. But listen. Your money is gone.

Scraps. Has it? Well, I'm not surprised.

Mr. B. You will be when you learn who took it. 'Twas Matthew Allen.

Scraps. You're mistaken. 'Twas the other.

Mr. B. What other?

Scraps. Richard Carnes.

Mr. B. No, Job, 'twas Matthew. Of that I am sure. He was left in charge of the office. He was seen in Murphy's billiard-room at nine o'clock. I'm sure. When I found the money gone this morning, I put a detective upon his track. There can be no mistake. It is Matthew Allen.

Scraps. I don't believe it. If forty detectives were on his track, if a thousand circumstances conspired to point out Matthew Allen as the thief, I would doubt all but his honesty.

Mr. B. Bah! Job, you're too credulous. He has been false to his trust. Against my express orders, he left my store last night; and should he ever return, I will discharge him from my employ.

Scraps. Don't be hasty, Abel. Give the lad a chance.

He has served you well. Even if he were guilty, you should be merciful.

Mr. B. Merciful to a thief? How do I know but what he has robbed me before? No, he shall be punished.

Scraps. Bah! You'll have to beg his pardon for suspecting him. Abel, keep cool. Wait till the real thief shows his hand.

Mr. B. He has shown it now. No, no, Job, you like the lad, and would save him if you could; but depend upon it (*Enter* RACHEL, R.) the thief who stole your money was Matthew Allen. (*Exit*, L.)

Rachel. O, what do I hear? Matthew suspected! No, no, it cannot be. Mr. Layton (*comes down* R. *of* SCRAPS), what did he say? What did he say? Whom does he suspect?

Scraps (*aside*). His sister! 'Twould break her heart. (*Aloud.*) Hey? You're on the wrong side. (*Crosses to* R.) I'll go and change this toggery, for I don't feel easy. (*Exit*, R.)

Rachel. Brother Mat suspected! O, I never thought of that. But I can clear him, I can clear him. But how? By denouncing Charley, my Charley, that I love so dearly? O, I can never do that. Perhaps he wanted the money for some special service. Perhaps — O, why should I try to excuse so base a deed? O, would that I were dead! If I betray Charley, his father will drive him from the house, and I should never see him again. And, spite of his crime, I love him so dearly! But my brother! He must not suffer for the crime of another, nor will he, for they have no proof. And Charley; he would curse me should I betray him. O, what shall I do! (*Falls on her knees by sofa.*) O, mother, sainted mother! if you watch over your child, guide her in this dark hour. (*Buries her head in sofa, weeping.*)

Enter RICHARD, R.

Rich. Ah, Shellie! at your devotions. (RACHEL *rises suddenly.*) Don't let me disturb you. Where are all the good people?

Rachel. Good evening, Mr. Carnes. Take a seat. Grace and my aunt will soon appear.

Rich. Thank you. (*Sits* L. *of table.* RACHEL *on lounge.*) Has Mat returned yet?

Rachel. No, we are expecting him every moment. I am sorry he could not arrive sooner.

Rich. (*aside*). So am I. I expected to find his coat hanging in the hall. Old Scraps's money-bag is heavy in my pocket and on my conscience. I must get it disposed of somewhere about Mat's wardrobe. (*Aloud.*) Where's Charley, Shellie?

Rachel. I don't know.

Enter CHARLEY, R.

Chas. Nor does she care, Dick. I'm glad to see you. Do you feel better, Shellie?

Rachel (*turns her back*). No, I don't feel better.

Chas. Then we must get Aunt Betsey to prescribe for you. (*Enter* BETSEY.) Here, Aunt Betsey, is another patient for you. Come, Shellie, tell her your symptoms.

Betsey. Symptoms! Well, if they're anything like

those of the last patient you found for me, I prescribe a lunatic asylum at once. How do you do, Mr. Carnes?

Rich. Good evening, Miss Benton. How becomingly you are dressed this evening! Your stately person —

Betsey. Now don't *you* be a fool. I've heard enough allusion to my personal appearance this evening already to make me sick. (*Sits* R. *of table.*)

Chas. (*aside*). Hullo! Scraps must have made a failure. (*Aloud.*) Did you comfort my friend, Mr. Layton, Aunt Betsey?

Betsey. You just bring him here again, that's all.

Enter GRACE, L.

Grace. Shellie, Shellie, Matthew's come. I heard his step on the walk — and I should know it — (*Stops confused.*) Why, I didn't know we had company. Good evening, Mr. Carnes.

Rich. Good evening, Miss Benton.

Grace (*aside*). Tiresome thing! Just spoiled my meeting Matthew in the hall. (*Aloud.*) Shellie, why don't you run and meet Matthew?

Rachel. My head aches fearfully. (*Aside.*) How can I meet him?

Betsey. Land sakes! He knows the way from cellar to garret.

Enter MATTHEW, R., *with coat on his arm, which he throws across chair*, R.

Mat. Ah, here you all are. Home again, as you see.

Grace (*running to him*). Matthew, welcome!

Mat. Thank you, my dear (*pause*), dear friend. (*Takes her hand.*)

Grace. Well, what success?

Mat. The best of success. The cargo of the Elmyra is sold. (*Enter* MR. BENTON, L.) Good evening, Mr. Benton. I was just telling your daughter my mission was successful. The cargo of the Elmyra has been taken.

Mr. B. Indeed. Do you know of anything else that has been taken, *Mr.* Allen?

Mat (*surprised*). Mr. Allen? To what do you allude, Mr. Benton?

Mr. B. Matthew Allen, as you well know, I am a man of very few words. Last night you were left in charge of my warehouse. During the night a bag of gold, placed in a drawer for safe keeping, was abstracted. Where is it?

Mat. A bag of gold, belonging to Job Layton, stolen? I know nothing about it.

Rachel (*aside*). Why don't Charley speak? (CHARLEY *is in conversation with* AUNT BETSEY.)

Mr. B. This is strange. You were left in charge of the warehouse. Did you leave it during the night?

Mat. I did.

Mr. B. Where did you go?

Mat. That, sir, I cannot tell. I received a note late in the evening from a friend, calling upon me as a friend to assist him. That is all I can say. It remains for him to clear the mystery.

Rachel (*aside*). O, why don't Charley speak? One word from him, and Matthew is clear.

Mr. B. So, sir, *you* cannot clear the mystery; but I can. You left that place to go to Murphy's billiard-room. You were seen there. This money was left in your charge. You alone were responsible for it; and I charge you with the theft.

Mat. Mr. Benton!

Grace. Father!

Rachel (*aside*). And there Charley sits as cool as a villain. Why don't he speak?

Mr. B. Yes, Matthew Allen, I have trusted you fully. I have believed in your truth and honesty; but the very fact that you quitted that store is proof positive of your guilt.

Mat. Mr. Benton, all I have in the world I owe to you. I believe I have not been ungrateful for your kindness. Had I done the base deed of which you accuse me, I could not look you in the face, as I do now, and pronounce your charge false.

Rachel (*jumping up.*) Charley Benton, do you hear? Why don't you speak?

Chas. I beg your pardon, Shellie. What's broke? I've been having a talk with Aunt Betsey.

Rachel. Mat, my brother Matthew, is accused of theft — by your father, too.

Chas. That's a serious matter. I say, father, what is it?

Mr. B. Nothing that should be made public. Matthew Allen is about to quit my service disgraced.

Mat. Disgraced?

Mr. B. Yes, disgraced! Everything is against you — your absence from the store, the empty drawer, the missing money-bag —

Chas. (*aside*). Drawer, store, money-bag! (*Aloud.*) I say, Shellie, what's all this?

Rachel. And you ask me? Shame, shame, Charley Benton.

Chas. Well, confound it! If you won't tell me what it's all about, you'll excuse me if I don't interfere. (*Retires up.*)

Mr. B. (*to* MATTHEW). There is not one circumstance in your favor.

Grace. Father, you are wrong. There are a thousand: his good, true life; his zeal in your service; his care for his sister; — all stand out to shield him from suspicion.

Mr. B. You, Grace, defend him?

Grace. With my life, if need be. I know him to be so good, so true, so noble, that when you turn him from your door, my arm shall be around him, and my voice shall whisper in his ear, " Whither thou goest I go."

Mat. Dear, dear Grace!

Rachel (*aside*). Must I learn my duty from her.

Mr. B. Never! No daughter of mine shall link her fate with a felon — a thief!

Grace. A thief? 'Tis false!

Rachel. Ay, false, false! And I can prove it.

All. You, Shellie? (AUNT BETSEY *comes down*, L. *Situations :* MATTHEW, R., GRACE, R. C., RACHEL, C., MR. BENTON, L. C., AUNT BETSEY, L., CHARLEY *and* RICHARD *back by the table, looking on.*)

Rachel. Yes, I ; for I was in the counting-room when that money was taken. My brother is guiltless. He was called to help a friend, as he tells you. I was left alone. I heard a step ; blew out the candle. The thief entered, opened the drawer in the table, moved away, and then returned and made a second attempt. I was so frightened that I did not tell my brother.

Mat. That was wrong, Shellie.

Rachel. I know it, brother. I have deceived you, and am no more worthy to be called your keeper. But you shall be cleared. (*With feeling.*) Uncle Abe, suppose a young girl had a brother, whom she loved very dearly ; a brother, whom she had told her dying mother, should never suffer, when any sacrifice could be made on her part. Suppose she also had a lover, whom she loved very dearly, — very, very dearly, — and she were called upon to sacrifice one or the other, who had committed a crime, what should you advise to do?

Mr. B. Save the innocent — if it broke her heart.

Rachel. Right, Uncle Abe ; you are right, sir. Listen, then. Last night, when that thief came in for the second time, I was on the alert. After he had accomplished his purpose, he struck a match, and as he held it up to light a cigar, I saw his face.

Mat. His face, Shellie? Did you know him?

Rachel. Know him? (*Throws herself into his arms.*) Too well, too well. 'Twas him. (*Pointing.*) Charley Benton.

All. Charley Benton ! (*All fall back, showing* CHARLEY *coolly seated on the table with his arms folded.*)

Chas. Well, what of it? I was in the store last night, did open the the drawer, and take from it —

Mr. B. The bag of gold?

Chas. (*coming down.*) No, sir, the pitcher's badge, which you so unceremoniously locked up for me.

Mr. B. But the money?

Chas. I know nothing about it. There was none there when I took the badge, that's certain.

Mat. So, Charley, your note to me was a blind to get me from the store.

Chas. What note? I sent no note. Hang it, what a mysterious time you are having here! Who's the robber, anyhow?

Mat. I received a note signed with the name of Charley Benton. Here it is. I thought it my duty to leave the store, as I had left my sister in charge.

Chas. And Shellie caught the thief?

Rachel. Stop, Charley. Did you take the badge the first or second time you entered the room?

Chas. Hang it, Shellie, are you beginning to be suspicious? I entered the store but once.

Rachel. And found nothing in the drawer but the badge?

Chas. Not a thing.

Rachel. Then there was another.

Rich. (aside). I wish I was well rid of this bag. There's Mat's coat in the chair. I can easily slip it into the pocket, and then I'm safe.

Mr. B. Yes, there was another; and that other your brother.

Grace. Still suspicious, father.

Mr. B. Still suspicious; and, until the thief is found, you, Matthew Allen, are suspended from service.

Mat. This is very hard, Mr. Benton.

Mr. B. You should not have left that store had fifty notes been sent you. Had the building been in flames you should not have disobeyed my orders.

Rich. (who has crept over to chair, R. Aside). Now, then, to fasten his guilt.

Mat. Very well, sir. I have tried to do my duty. If I have failed, my heart, my conscience acquit me of blame or guilt. ·

Rich. (*takes money-bag from his breast pocket. Aside*). All right. Now, then. (*About to place it in* MATTHEW'S *coat pocket.* SCRAPS *enters suddenly,* R., *in his old costume, his basket in both hands.*)

Scraps. Hey? (*Holds out basket.* RICHARD *starts back, and drops the bag into basket.*) You're on the wrong side, Mr. Carnes, the wrong side. · ·

Mr. B. Job Layton, what are you doing? ·· ··

· *Scraps.* Recovering my money. Here it is. · (*Comes down,* C.) Here is the money (*showing basket*), and here the thief. (*Seizing* RICHARD *by wrist.*) : ·

Mr. B. Richard Carnes? You are mistaken, Job.

Scraps. Now don't be a fool, Abel. I knew when I placed that money in your hands it would be found in the possession of Richard Carnes. He's a notorious gambler; that I know. He frequents Murphy's billiard-rooms; he was there last night; wrote a note to Matthew Allen, and sent it to the store last night; then entered the store with a false key — O, I know him! I've proof enough that he committed this theft to put him in prison, and he knows it. Hey, Mr. Carnes?

Mr. B. Richard Carnes, what have you to say?

Rich. Nothing: if you take the word of that ragamuffin, I am a thief; but this little affair was arranged for an entirely different purpose. It has failed, and I am the loser. I am a gentleman's son; my father will make all losses good. As for the business, I have grown tired of it, and want a change; so, with your permission, I will throw up my situation. If I am wanted, you will find me at home. I shall not run away. Good evening, Mr. Benton; good evening, all. (*At door*, R.) A cursed stupid mess I've made of it. (*Exit*, R.)

Scraps. Well, that's cool.

Chas. Decidedly. Shall I stop him, father?

Mr. B. No; let him go. If he feels one half the shame I feel for my share in this business, he is sufficiently punished. (*Crosses to* MATTHEW.) Matthew, I beg your pardon. I have been hasty. Knowing your worth, I should have cut my tongue out ere I made the charge I did.

Mat. Let it pass, Mr. Benton. Circumstances were against me. I should not have left your store; and the fear of compromising your son kept me silent.

Mr. B. And you (*to* CHARLEY), what have you to say for your share in this?

Chas. Me? Well, I like that! It strikes me I'm the martyr — suspected of being a thief, and by Shellie, too.

Rachel. O Charley, forgive me. I thought I was right. It was my brother —

Chas. O, well, if a brother is to stand between you and me, the sooner I claim the privileges of a husband the better.

Betsey. Shellie, that man in the ragged coat! Bless my soul, it's him — the man that saved me from the runaway horse.

Rachel. Why, so it is. Strange I should not have recognized him.

Betsey. Who is he? What's his name?

4

Chas. Why, don't you know? That's Job Layton, Esq.

Betsey. What, the lunatic? Well, if I'd have known he was my preserver — Mr. Layton, Mr. Layton?

Scraps. Hey? You're on the wrong side. (*Turns his back to her.*)

Chas. It's no use, Aunt Betsey. You've lost your chance.

Grace. And now, father, where is the new partner you were to present this evening?

Mr. B. He is here. (*Places his hand on* MATTHEW'S *shoulder.*) Matthew Allen, for your long service, for your true, earnest zeal, for your honesty and value, I offer you a partnership.

Mat. Me? O, Mr. Benton, you are my best friend, but I cannot accept.

Mr. B. Not accept?

Mat. No, sir, for I have already formed a partnership with another — this dear girl.

Grace. Yes, father, we have formed a partnership for life.

Mr. B. I see; and, though I have not been asked, I will give my consent. Have your partner, but he must also be mine, under the firm of Abel Benton & Son.

Chas. Well, it strikes me I shall be left out in the cold.

Mr. B. Your turn shall come next, with Matthew's consent.

Mat. Anything you wish, sir.

Rachel. But what's to become of me?

Chas. Now don't you fret about that, Shellie. Grace

is going into the new firm. Let's you and I form an opposition.

Rachel. And so Miss Grace is to usurp my place. Well, I suppose I must bear it.

Scraps. Shellie, that scamp of a Charley wants a keeper. I know him. He's a rascal — jumps into the water, you know. Marry him, and watch him.

Rachel. What do you say, Uncle Abe?

Mr. B. You have my full consent.

Rachel. And you, brother Mat?

Mat. I know no one more worthy of my dear sister than Charley Benton.

Rachel. There's my hand, Charley. And as I have tried to be true to my brother, so may I be true to you. If I have failed in my duty there, it was for love of you.

Mat. Nay, nay, Sunshine; you have been ever true. The happiness of this hour I owe to you alone.

Rachel. Say, rather, to our dear, trusty, watchful old rag-picker.

Scraps. Hey? You're on the wrong side. Earthly friends may do much to guide and guard each other, but Justice, Love, and Truth are servants of a higher Power, who, in the darkest hour, is ever the sure, safe, reliant keeper.

Disposition of Characters.

R.   C.   L.

SCRAPS.

GRACE.   CHARLEY.

MATTHEW.   RACHEL.

MR. BENTON.   BETSEY.

www.ingramcontent.com/pod-product-compliance
Lightning Source LLC
Chambersburg PA
CBHW021227260626
47172CB00002B/649